W9-AVL-964

Copyright © 1990 by Kady MacDonald Denton

All rights reserved. No part of this book may
be reproduced in any form or by any electronic or
mechanical means, including information storage
and retrieval systems, without permission in
writing from the publisher, except by a reviewer
who may quote brief passages in a review.

First edition

Published in Great Britain in 1990 by
Methuen Children's Books

ISBN 0-316-18091-2
Library of Congress Catalog Card Number 89-43566
Library of Congress Cataloging-in-Publication information is available.

10 9 8 7 6 5 4 3 2 1

Published simultaneously in Canada
by Little, Brown & Company (Canada) Limited

Printed in England

THE CHRISTMAS BOOT

Kady MacDonald Denton

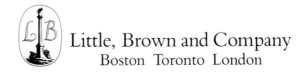
Little, Brown and Company
Boston Toronto London

One cold day in December, a few days after
Christmas, Alison found a black, shiny boot.
"Look," she called to Jeremy, "come and see.
There's a boot in the tree."

"I'll try it on," said Jeremy.
"This isn't right," he said. "The boot's too tight.
There's something stuck in the toe."
"Oh, look!" they cried. "It's a little red ball."

"Here's a spinning top!" said Alison.

"And here's a tiny horse," shouted Jeremy.
"It must be a magic boot!"

"We'll keep the boot," said Jeremy.

"I'll keep the boot. Give it to me," said Alison.

Jeremy and Alison both grabbed the boot
and as they pulled, more presents fell out.
"Look!" shouted Alison.

"Presents!" Alison and Jeremy called
to the other children in the park.
"Look! Presents for everyone!"

"Whose boot is it?" asked the children.
"I don't know," said Jeremy. "Someone has lost
a boot and some presents."

"It's a man's boot," said Alison. "Who do we know
with big winter boots and lots of presents?"

"Santa Claus!" shouted all the children.
"Then," said Alison, "we must give it back."
"But how can we give it back?" asked the children.

"What comes down, must go up," said Alison.
"We need a chimney. Come on, let's go to my house."

Alison told her mom that they wanted to leave
Santa's boot by the chimney.

Mom turned out the light. They shut their eyes,
as though it were Christmas Eve.
In the dark, all the children pretended to be asleep.

When the children opened their eyes . . .

the boot was gone!

They all rushed outside to see if they
could find Santa Claus.
"He's already gone," said Jeremy.
"Goodbye, Santa!" said Alison.
"Thank you," called their friends.
"Goodbye. Goodbye."